Cinderella

Story by:
Charles Perrault

Adapted by:
Margaret Ann Hughes

Illustrated by:
Russell Hicks
Douglas McCarthy
Theresa Mazurek
Allyn Conley-Gorniak
Julie Ann Armstrong

This Book Belongs To:

Use this symbol to match book and cassette.

Once upon a time, in a Chateau in the country, a young girl named Ella lived with her stepmother and her two stepsisters, Zelda and Aralia. Now most stepmothers are very nice, but this one was not nice at all. She was cruel to Ella and made her wear tattered rags and sleep in a bed of straw in the attic. And…she made her clean the house and cook the meals. When poor, tired Ella was finished, she would sit in a corner by the kitchen fire to keep warm. And because often she got dirty from the soot and cinders there, they called her "Cinderella."

Now the king of the land had an only son who was just the right age to marry.

So that a suitable bride could be found for his son, the king decided to hold a royal ball.
Now a ball is a great party where everyone wears their best clothes. There would be dancing and plenty of food.

Nigel, the king's messenger, delivered the invitations all across the land.
His last stop was the Chateau.

Cinderella was sweeping the floor when the invitation arrived. The stepsisters pushed and shoved their way to the front door.

The two girls grabbed the invitation from Nigel and tugged and pulled on it, until…

…the invitation tore in half.

The stepmother put the two pieces together and read the invitation out loud. It said that the ball was to be held that night at the king's castle, and all eligible young ladies were encouraged to attend.

Cinderella was just as excited as her stepsisters when she heard the news. She began dancing around the room with the broom as her partner.

Cinderella's stepmother and stepsisters kept her so busy getting them ready, that she didn't have time to think about herself. She filled their tubs with bath water, did their hair, then pressed their dresses. Then she hurried to her room in the attic and searched desperately for something she could wear to the ball.

Cinderella grabbed an old dress and held it tightly in her hands as she raced downstairs.

Cinderella's stepmother and stepsisters laughed and laughed and laughed at the idea of Cinderella going to the ball.

They closed the door behind them, leaving Cinderella alone in the quiet house.

Cinderella ran to her corner in the kitchen and cried and cried!

Just then, one of
Cinderella's tears fell
to the floor and began
to glow. The light grew
bigger and brighter,
until the light changed
into a shape, and the shape
became…a little old woman.

A fairy godmother! Cinderella
told her how she had been so busy
getting her stepsisters ready for
the ball.

The fairy godmother took
Cinderella by the hand and
led her into the garden.

Cinderella did as her fairy godmother asked and gathered up the pumpkin and the six mice, while her fairy godmother searched and searched for her wand. She finally found it in her pocket.

As the fairy godmother waved her wand, everything glowed with a radiant, magical light. The pumpkin became a golden coach, the mice became six gray prancing horses, and the rats became the coachman and the footman.

With a little magic, Cinderella was ready for the ball. She now wore a beautiful gown, and on her feet were two glass slippers.

The footman held open the carriage door, and Cinderella stepped inside.

The fairy godmother told Cinderella that she must be home by midnight, for at the stroke of twelve, the coach would turn back into a pumpkin, the horses back into mice, and the coachman and footman back into white rats.

The coachman gave the signal to the horses, and the coach took off towards the castle.

At the castle, the king was having a wonderful time trying to pick out a bride for his son. But the prince just wasn't having any fun at all.

Suddenly…a hush came over the ballroom. All eyes turned to the top of the staircase as Cinderella appeared. The prince couldn't take his eyes off her. He met her at the foot of the stairs.

He took her hand, and as the orchestra began to play, they danced and danced. They danced through the corridor and out onto the terrace beneath the starlit sky.

Cinderella and the prince were together all night long. The prince showed not a bit of interest in anyone else. Cinderella's stepsisters were very jealous.

It was almost twelve o'clock but Cinderella hadn't noticed the time, until she heard the bell in the clock tower.

Cinderella gave the prince a last fond look, then hurried away down the long corridor, to the ballroom, then down the outside staircase. The prince ran after her. Cinderlla ran so quickly, that she stumbled and lost one of her glass slippers on the stairs.

The clock struck ten!

Without stopping for her slipper, she ran faster and faster to her waiting coach.

Eleven!

She climbed in the coach and off it went.

Twelve!

But it was too late. The coach turned back into a pumpkin, and the mice and rats scurried away into the darkness. Cinderella found herself on the ground in her tattered rags, and she ran off into the night. When the prince reached the top of the stairs, he saw the glass slipper. He stopped, picked it up, then held it close to his heart.

As Cinderella ran home, she held tight to the remaining glass slipper. Her godmother had let her keep it to remember her wonderful evening with the prince.

She reached the Chateau just minutes before her stepmother and stepsisters. She hid the glass slipper in her pocket and ran to her corner near the fire, just as they walked in the door.

The two stepsisters and stepmother went off to bed, and Cinderella climbed the stairs to the attic, smiling and humming. No one, other than the prince, was more in love that night.

The next day the prince gave Nigel the glass slipper and sent him out into the kingdom to find the girl whose foot would fit it. The slipper was so dainty, that it fit none of the young ladies he tried it on.

Oh dear! Poor Nigel searched the countryside…

…and his last stop and last hope was the Chateau. Cinderella answered the door.

The stepsisters pushed Cinderella out of the way.

Nigel entered the Chateau with the glass slipper. He tried the slipper on Zelda first…

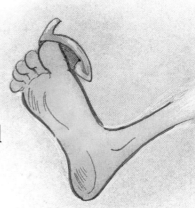

…but Zelda's foot was just too big.

Aralia's foot was much too fat.

Cinderella stepped forward to try the slipper. Nigel
eagerly knelt down and slipped the glass slipper
onto Cinderella's dainty foot. It fit perfectly. Then
Cinderella removed the other slipper from her
pocket and put it on, too.

Nigel knew he had found the right girl at last. Cinderella was taken to the castle, and there she was married to the prince. Her stepmother, Zelda and Aralia were welcome to visit the castle whenever they wished. You see, Cinderella had a good heart, and she forgave them for everything.

 nd they all lived happily ever after.